Patton, G

D0486947

STARS

to the playground

to Sam's house

to Con's house

2

to Emily's house

Lin's apartment

Mrs Mac's farm

3

Hi. My name is Lin and these are my friends. Today we are visiting Mrs Mac's Farm.

Mrs Mac

me (Lin)

Veronica Pickles

Toola
Oola

Emily
Rimmerly

5

Chapter 1
Milking the Cow

'First we need to milk Bessy,'
says Mrs Mac.
'Milk Bessy?' says Emily Rimmerly.
'I thought milk came in a bottle.'
We say, 'Emily Rimmerly, you are
so funny.'

'I was only joking,' says Emily.
'*Sure*, Emily,' we say.

'Emily Rimmerly, you can milk
the cow,' says Mrs Mac.
Emily squirts milk on her face.
Emily squirts milk on my face.

We say, 'Emily, the milk goes
into the bucket.' We say, 'Maybe
Mrs Mac should milk the cow.'
She does.

Emily says she doesn't want to
be a farmer when she grows up.
Mrs Mac smiles.

Chapter 2
Collecting Eggs

'Now it's time to collect the eggs from
the hen house,' says Mrs Mac.
'Collect eggs?' says Toola Oola.
'I thought eggs came in a carton.'
We say, 'Toola Oola, you are *so* funny.'

'I was only joking,' says Toola Oola.
'*Sure*, Toola,' we say.

'Toola Oola, you can collect the eggs,'
says Mrs Mac.
Toola looks next to the cockerel. No eggs.
Toola looks under the cockerel.

We say, 'Toola Oola, you won't
find any eggs there!'
We say, 'Maybe Mrs Mac should
collect the eggs.'
She does.

Toola says she doesn't want to be
a farmer when she grows up.
Mrs Mac smiles.

Chapter 3
Picking Peas

'It's time to pick the peas,'
says Mrs Mac.
'Pick peas?' says Veronica Pickles.
'I thought peas came in a bag.'
We say, 'Veronica Pickles, you are
so funny.'

'I was only joking,' says Veronica Pickles.
'*Sure*, Veronica,' we say.

'Veronica, you can pick the peas,'
says Mrs Mac.
Veronica looks in the trees. No peas.
Veronica looks under the ground.
No peas.

We say, 'Veronica Pickles, peas
don't grow under the ground.'
We say, 'Maybe Mrs Mac should
pick the peas.'
She does.

Veronica Pickles says she doesn't want
to be a farmer when she grows up.
Mrs Mac smiles.

Chapter 4
Finding the Potatoes

'Next it's time to find the potatoes,'
says Mrs Mac.
'Find potatoes?' I say.
'I thought potatoes came in a sack.'
'Lin, you are *so* funny,' say Toola Oola,
Veronica Pickles and
Emily Rimmerly.

'I was only joking,' I say.
'*Sure*, Lin,' they say.

'Lin, you can find the potatoes,'
says Mrs Mac.
I look under the hens. No potatoes.
I look under the ground. I find
potatoes — and they are very dirty!

Toola, Veronica and Emily say,
'Maybe Mrs Mac should pick
the potatoes.'
She does.

I say I don't want to be a farmer
when I grow up.
Mrs Mac smiles.

Chapter 5
A Farm Breakfast

'It's time for breakfast,' says Mrs Mac. We say we thought breakfast came from a cereal box!

'You girls are *so* funny,' says Mrs Mac. 'We were only joking,' we say. '*Sure*,' she says.

We all help make the breakfast.
Emily pours the milk.
Toola cooks the eggs.
Veronica shells the peas.
I cook the potatoes.

We have green peas, potato cakes and
scrambled eggs for breakfast. And a big
glass of milk.

Mrs Mac says that we make a very good farm breakfast. We say, 'Maybe we *will* be farmers when we grow up.'

And Mrs Mac smiles.

Survival Tips

Tips for surviving the farm

 **1** Stay in bed until 11 a.m.

 **2** Stay in bed all day. You won't have to go to the farm at all!

 **3** Move to the city.

4 Milk in the eye is no fun – wear glasses if you are milking!

5 Don't look for eggs under the cockerel. The cockerel will think you are very silly – and so will everyone else.

Riddles and Jokes

Veronica   What do you get from
               a nervous cow?
Lin   Milk shakes.

Emily   Why did the potatoes cry?
Toola   Because the chips were down.

Lin   Why don't eggs tell each
               other jokes?
Emily   They crack each other up.

Veronica   What has four legs and
               says 'boo'?
Toola   A cow with a cold.